HORSES

PINTO HORSES

JANET L. GAMMIE

ABDO & Daughters

Published by Abdo & Daughters, 4940 Viking Drive, Suite 622, Edina, Minnesota 55435.

Library bound edition distributed by Rockbottom Books, Pentagon Tower, P.O. Box 36036, Minneapolis, Minnesota 55435.

Printed in the United States.

Cover Photo credit: Peter Arnold, Inc.

Interior Photo credits: Julie Green

Edited by Bob Italia

Library of Congress Cataloging-in-Publication Data

Gammie, Janet L.
    Pinto Horses/ Janet L. Gammie.
        p.   cm. — (Horses)
Includes bibliographical references (p.23) and index.
    ISBN 1-56239-439-8
1. Pinto horse—Juvenlle literature. [l. Pinto horse. 2. Horses.] I. Title. II. Series: Gammie, Janet L. Horses.
SF293.P5G36 1995
636.1'3—dc20   95-2240
                                                                    CIP
                                                                    AC

ABOUT THE AUTHOR

Janet Gammie has worked with thoroughbred race horses for over 10 years. She trained and galloped thoroughbred race horses while working on the racetracks and farms in Louisiana and Arkansas. She is a graduate of Louisiana Tech University's Animal Science program with an equine specialty.

Contents

WHERE PINTOS CAME FROM

Horses are mammals just like humans. Mammals are warm-blooded animals with a backbone. Their body heat comes from inside their body.

The horses earliest **ancestor** was *Eohippus* (e-oh-HIP-us). It lived about 50 million years ago and was 12 inches (30 cm) high. The Spanish brought pintos to America

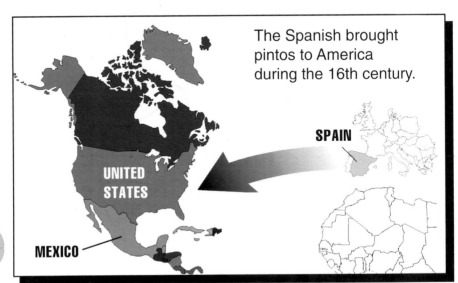

The Spanish brought pintos to America during the 16th century.

SPAIN

UNITED STATES

MEXICO

Detail Area

The pinto is a spotted horse.

from Spain during the 16th century.

Pinto is the Spanish word for *paint* or *spotted.* The Spanish horses were then **bred** with the American mustang. In time Native Americans **tamed** the pintos. They are best known as the Native American horses of the Old West.

WHAT PINTOS LOOK LIKE

Pintos are not a true horse breed. They are a color breed. A true breed is a group of horses or ponies that are of one family, like the **thoroughbred**. A color breed can be made up of many different horse families. But it must have a special color pattern.

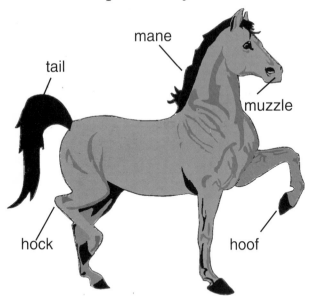

Pintos come from stock, light horse or pony breeds. Stock horses are **quarter horses** and thoroughbreds.

A light horse breed is any true horse breed other than quarter horse and thoroughbred.

Horses share the same features.

Pintos are a color breed.

Pintos can be 12 to 17 hands high (hh). Each hand equals 4 inches (10 centimeters). Pintos can be any shape or size. They can be small like a pony or tall like a **thoroughbred**.

WHAT MAKES PINTOS SPECIAL

Breeding will decide a pinto's quality and type. If it has **quarter horse** breeding it will have big muscles and good balance. If it has pony breeding it will be small and sturdy.

A pinto can also have **saddlebred** breeding. A saddlebred can be three-gaited or five-gaited. Gaited means the way a horse moves its **hooves**.

Saddlebreds bring their knees and hooves high off the ground when they walk or trot. This is called high action. This high action gives a smooth ride. If a pinto has saddlebred breeding it will have high action and give a smooth ride.

Pintos give a rider a smooth ride with high action.

COLOR

There are two basic color types for pintos: piebald and skewbald. Piebald is a horse that is black with white spots. Skewbald is a horse that is white with any color except black.

Pintos have two color patterns: overo and tobiano (toe-be-AH-no). Overo pintos are colored horses with uneven white spots. The white cannot cross the back. Their tails must be one color. Blue (glass) eyes are common. Tobiano horses are white with colored spots. The regular white spots can cross the back. Their tails are two-toned. Their eyes are often dark.

Pinto markings are a solid white color patch on the head and legs. A pinto with a white face is called a bald face. It is the most common head marking for overos.

This pinto is skewbald which means it is white with different colored spots.

Overos have at least one dark or spotted leg. Tobianos can have any head markings except bald face. All four legs must be white to the knee and hock. The hock is the knee joint on the rear legs.

CARE

To protect horses from disease and sickness they are vaccinated (VAK-sin-ay-ted) often. A vaccination is a shot that helps prevent disease.

Regular **deworming** keeps the horse free of parasites inside its body. A parasite is a bug that lives off another animal. These bugs live on plants and grass. The horse swallows the parasites when eating.

Parasites also live on the outside of the horse. They cling to and feed on the hair and skin. Daily **grooming** keeps away these parasites.

Grooming also makes the horse feel good. Horses are brushed with many different brush types. Brushes can be soft, hard, plastic, or rubber.

Horses like to be brushed. When they are kept in stalls they can become bored. They welcome the company. Horses are brushed before and after riding. This stops saddle sores. Their **hooves** are picked with a hoof pick.

Pintos like to be brushed. Grooming makes them feel good.

FEEDING

Horses are fed different amounts of feed, depending on age, growth and whether they are **pregnant**. Feed includes hay, grains and water. Hays are grasses and **alfalfa**.

There are many grass types. Each type offers different **nutrition**. Alfalfa is higher in **protein** than the grasses. If a horse is fed too much alfalfa it will become sick.

Grains include oats, wheat, barley, and corn. Different grain amounts are fed depending on how active the horse is and how much it has grown. Fresh, clean water should always be given. After training, give the horse a little water so it does not get sick.

Pintos, like all horses, eat hay and grass.

THINGS PINTOS NEED

The saddle protects a horse's back and makes riding easier. The first padded saddle came from the **Ukraine** in Russia. The **Mongolians** developed the stirrup many years ago. Stirrups are the part of the saddle where you place your feet.

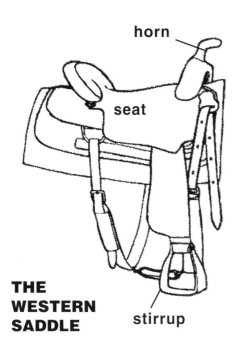

horn

seat

THE WESTERN SADDLE

stirrup

Today there are two basic types of saddles: the **Western saddle** and the **English saddle**. Each saddle type has many designs. How the horse is used will decide the saddle type and design.

There are also Western and English **bridles** and **bits**. The horse's behavior during **training** will decide which bit is used.

*The saddle protects the pinto's back and
makes riding easier.*

HOW PINTOS GROW

A **foal** lives inside the **mare's** body for about 11 months. At birth the foal can see and hear. It takes the foal about 15 minutes to stand after it is born. The foal can live without the mare's milk after 3 to 4 months.

About five months after birth, the foal is taken away from the mare. This is called weaning. The foal is then called a weanling.

Weanlings are kept together in one **pasture** where they play, sleep and eat. Playing keeps the weanlings strong and healthy. It also forms skills the horse will need all of its life.

A foal can stand about 15 minutes after it is born.

TRAINING

Training begins when the **foal** is taught to wear a **halter** and to lead. Leading is walking beside a person while on a rope—like a dog walking on a leash. It is easier for and kinder to a horse to learn basic commands at a young age.

Ground training begins at one or two years of age. Ground training is the lessons a horse learns before it is saddled and ridden.

Horses should not carry an adult's weight until they are at least two years old. Until that time their bones are growing and are easily injured. When the two-year-old horse has accepted the saddle and rider, it can begin its next training stage.

Training begins early with a foal. They learn basic commands at a young age.

GLOSSARY

ALFALFA - Any group of plants resembling clover, many of which are grown as food for cattle.

ANCESTOR (AN-ses-tor) - An animal from which other animals are descended.

BIT - The metal piece of a bridle that goes in the horse's mouth.

BREED - To produce young; also, a group of animals that look alike and have the same ancestor.

BRIDLE - The part of the harness that fits over the horse's head (including the bit and reins), used to guide or control the animal.

DEWORMING (de-WURM-ing) - To take away worms.

DISEASE - An illness caused by a virus.

ENGLISH SADDLE - A flat-seated saddle used for racing, and sporting.

EQUIPMENT (e-QWIP-ment) - Saddles and bridles.

EXTERNAL (eks-TUR-nal) - On the outside.

FOAL - A young horse under one year old.

GROOM - To clean and brush.

HALTER - A strap used for leading or tying an animal. It fits around the animal's nose and over or behind its ears.

HOOF - A horse's foot.

INTERNAL (in-TUR-nal) - On the inside.

MARE - A female horse.

MONGOLIA (mong-GO-le-a) - A place in East-central Asia.

NUTRITION (noo-TRISH-in) - The use of food for energy.

PASTURE - A field used for the grazing of cattle, sheep, or other animals.

PREGNANT - With one or more babies growing inside the body.

PROTEIN - A substance containing nitrogen which is a necessary part of plant and animal cells.

QUARTER HORSE - A compact muscular saddle horse that can run at high speed for short distances.

SADDLEBRED - A horse that is bred for riding.

TAME - Taken from the wild and made obedient.

THOROUGHBRED - A horse descended from a breed first developed at the end of the eighteenth century by crossing English mares with Arabian stallions. They are trained for horse racing.

TRAINING - To teach.

UKRAINE (yoo-KRAYN) - An area of Russia.

WESTERN SADDLE - A strong saddle used by cowboys.

BIBLIOGRAPHY

Millar, Jane. *Birth of a Foal.* J. B. Lippincott Company, New York, 1977.

Patent, Dorothy Hinshaw. *A Horse of a Different Color.* Dodd, Mead and Company, New York, 1988.

———.*Horses of America*, Holiday House, New York, 1981.

Possell, Elsa. *Horses.* Childrens Press, Chicago, 1961.

Index